Super Spooked

written by Gina Bellisario

illustrated by Jessika von Innerebner

raintree
a Capstone company — publishers for children

CONTENTS

CHAPTER 1

A bad dream

It was just another day in the city of Winkopolis. Zombies moaned. Ghosts wailed. Skeletons rattled. Everyone was doing the same old ordinary things. Everyone, mind you, but the girl who lived at 8 Louise Lane.

That girl was Ellie Ultra. It was the night before Halloween, and she was getting ready for bed faster than a witch on a jet-powered broomstick. It was *extra*ordinary.

Whoosh! Ellie flew over to her Princess Power lamp and turned it on. She smiled as the statue of the comic book princess lit up brightly. Then she switched off the main light before hopping under her duvet.

"Lights out, my super girl," Mum said, popping into Ellie's room. "Do-gooders need a good night's sleep." She walked over to the Princess Power lamp and reached to turn it off.

Ellie sat up straight. "Don't turn off my Princess Power light! It saves me from the dark."

"The dark?" Mum folded her arms and frowned. "Since when do you need rescuing from that?"

"Since yesterday," Ellie admitted. "I had a really bad dream. I think my comic book

spooked me." She motioned to *Princess Power, Protector of Sparkle Kingdom: Creature in the Castle*, which was lying on her bed.

Mum moved the comic book aside and sat next to Ellie. "What was the dream about?" she asked.

"The lights went out, and I was standing all alone," Ellie began. "Suddenly the dark shadows turned into a terrible beast! It had pointy fangs and hair that poked out everywhere. It stared at me with glowing eyes." She shivered and pulled the covers up to her chin. "The dark was going to gobble me up!"

"It was only a dream," Mum said, smoothing Ellie's hair. "Besides, you can stand up to your fear. You've tackled tough problems before. Remember the super-villains you've fought?"

Memories of villains from her past flashed like fireworks in Ellie's mind. There was Boo Hoo, the ghost who cried and cried until Ellie let him have her brand new Cupcake Friends pencil top. There was also the Green-Eyed Goblin. He was always after Ellie's things such as her chocolate-chip pancakes.

"Battling villains *is* hard," Ellie agreed. "But fighting the dark is impossible! I can't outrun it with my super speed. I can't crush it with my super strength. Even my X-ray vision and invisibility powers are useless."

Mum smiled encouragingly. "You don't need superpowers to fight your fear. You just have to face it. Then you'll see it's not that scary."

"I suppose. . ." Ellie replied. But she still thought the dark wanted her for dinner.

"Let's give it a try." Mum leaned over and turned the lamp off. Princess Power faded until the room was as inky black as her trusty steed, Steel Blossom.

Ellie immediately hid under the covers.

"Ellie, look around," Mum instructed.

"No way!" Ellie exclaimed. "I'd rather battle a franken-fish."

"Don't be afraid," Mum said, giving Ellie a gentle nudge. "Tell me, what can you see?"

Slowly, Ellie lowered her duvet and gazed around the dark room. It was full of odd shapes. She knew they were only her clothes and other belongings, but the dark made everything seem scary.

Her cape, which was hanging on her desk chair, looked like a flying ghost. Pens, which were sticking out of a mug, looked like spikes on a dragon's tail. Through the wardrobe doors, two yellow lights glowed. Ellie moved left, then right, trying to work out what they were coming from. But they only followed her like hungry eyes.

Ellie gulped. "Something is watching me," she told Mum, pointing at the lights. "It must be the dark. It's waiting to swallow me whole!"

Mum walked over to the wardrobe and pulled out an electronic toy owl. "It's just your talking Hoot-Hoot doll," she said. She pressed a button on its belly, and the owl's eyes stopped glowing. "I know it can be easy to let your fear take control. But our fears get power from us. We can take that power back. We can choose not to be afraid."

With that, she kissed Ellie's forehead and left the room.

Ellie could feel the darkness surround her. It was going to strike, no doubt. She took a deep breath, trying to gather her strength.

"I'm not afraid," she said. "I can fight anything – outer space blobs, mad scientists, comic book villains – even my fear."

Suddenly the door opened. Seconds later, a strange sound hit Ellie's supersonic ears. *Sniff-sniff, sniff-sniff.* She glanced over and noticed a shadow on the wall. The shadow was shaped like a beast, with wild hair and craggy teeth.

It was the monster from her dream! Ellie was sure of it. The darkness had sniffed her out, and now it was going to turn her into a bedtime snack!

"I am not afraid. I am not afraid. I am not afraid . . ." Ellie repeated as the shadow moved towards her. Her heart started to beat at turbo speed when – *THUMP!* – something jumped on the end of the bed.

Lightning-fast, Ellie bolted out of bed. She shot across the floor, knocking over an easel and some paintbrushes. Clenching her fists, she activated her heating power.

"Stand back, darkness!" she warned as her hands flared like fireballs. "I'll fry you to a crisp!" She spun around to face her foe and gasped.

"Ruff!" barked Super Fluffy, Ellie's puppy pal. He was standing on Ellie's bed, wagging his tail playfully.

In an instant, Ellie's fiery hands fizzled out, and she sighed with relief. "Fluffster, you nearly scared the stuffing out of me! I thought you were a villain."

Super Fluffy let out a small whimper.

"Never mind." Ellie put her easel and brushes away, then picked up her pooch. "It's time to go to sleep," she said, placing him on his doggy bed in the corner. "I've had enough excitement for one night. And besides, I have to get up for school in the morning."

Super Fluffy curled up on his bed. In no time, he was sound asleep. Apparently he wasn't scared of the dark. In fact, it didn't seem to bother him at all.

After she had switched her Princess Power lamp back on, Ellie returned to bed.

If I was stronger than my fear, it wouldn't frighten me, Ellie thought as she dozed off. But the dark was a powerful enemy. More powerful than any super-villain she'd faced. Ellie wasn't sure if even her superpowers could help her to conquer it.

CHAPTER 2

Super Chicken

At school the next day, the dining hall was alive with Halloween spirit. Paper-plate bats decorated the walls. Under the clock, a statue of Frankenstein's monster held a menu. Today's lunch was *Spook-ghetti* and *Boo-berry Pie*.

Flying inside, Ellie giggled at a funny cardboard ghost above the door. *It's not scary in here,* she thought. *I could stand up to this stuff any day. But the dark? No way!*

Just then, Ellie's best friend, Hannah, ran over carrying her tray. On her plate, a round pizza was smiling like a pumpkin.

"Look what I've got – a jack-o'-lantern pizza!" Hannah said. "And did you see that decoration?" She nodded at the wall behind the lunch counter, where a stringy cobweb stretched from the floor to the ceiling. Sitting in the middle of the web was a giant inflatable spider.

Ellie's eyes bulged at the eight-legged monster. "Wow! It looks like Itsy Bitsy, the three-metre-tall spider," she replied as they headed for the back table. Amanda and Payton were already waiting. "Last year, that villain tried to climb the Winkopolis water tower."

At the table, Hannah twirled around once before putting her tray next to Amanda's. "Ballet is cancelled today because of Halloween, so I'd better squeeze in some practice," she said. "There's a big performance coming up. I don't want to forget my routine!" She pointed her toes and gracefully lifted her leg behind her.

The girls clapped as Hannah took her seat. "You'll be great!" said Amanda. "You practise so much, even I know your routine!"

"My football practice was cancelled too," Payton said. "Do you know what that means? More time to trick-or-treat together!"

"Let's meet at my house after school," said Hannah. "I can't wait to dress up. I'm going to be a ballerina, so I'm wearing the costume from my dance performance." She turned to Ellie. "Are you dressing up as a superhero, Ellie? You won't even need a costume!"

Ellie smiled and shook her head. She was hanging up her cape for Halloween. Even superheroes needed a day off.

"I've decided to be a scientist like my mum and dad," she replied. "I'm borrowing my mum's lab coat, but she has to wash it first. She spilled flower formula on herself. Now her coat is bright yellow – and it smells like a daisy."

"Whoops! I'd better tidy myself up too," Amanda said, looking down at her T-shirt. She had squeezed her juice carton too hard, and juice had squirted all over her.

Ellie leaped from her seat. "I'll get napkins. Be back in a flash!"

Racing past the tables, she hurried to the other side of the lunch counter. As she grabbed napkins from the basket, she felt something above her and looked up.

The inflatable spider was staring down threateningly.

Good thing it's not the real Itsy Bitsy, Ellie thought. *Or it might eat the Year 5 teacher, Mr Fly.*

Just then, a werewolf in trainers jumped in front of Ellie. Fake fangs stuck out of its mouth. "Boo!" it shouted.

Surprised, Ellie flew back against the cobweb. A string caught her shoe, ensnaring her. "This trap can't hold me!" she said defiantly. She tugged on the string and pulled herself free.

Suddenly – *Ping! Ping! Ping!* – the hooks that held up the decoration popped out of the ceiling. It went crashing to the floor. The spider lay upside down on the ground. Its eight legs stuck out from a pile of tangled strings.

Ellie's cheeks got red as everyone in the room turned and pointed. She had made a monster mess!

"I totally scared you!" Dex Diggs, Ellie's arch-enemy, cheered. He took off his werewolf mask and howled with laughter. "Maybe I should call you Super Chicken? Or . . . I know! What about Captain Cluck?" Flapping his arms, he clucked like a chicken.

Ellie glared at Dex. She should've known he would play a trick on her today. Using her mind-reading power, she learned this wasn't the end of his evil high jinks. He was planning to surprise her again while she was out trick-or-treating.

Dex loves ruffling my feathers, she thought.

Ellie left Dex strutting in circles and went to fix the decoration. "Sorry, Mr Arachnid," she said. "My muscles are mightier than I thought." She untangled the strings from its legs. Then she zipped up to the ceiling and re-hung everything.

With the spider back in its web, Ellie returned to her table and delivered the napkins to Amanda. "I would've brought these sooner if it hadn't been for Dex," she said.

"That troublemaker won't ruin our day," Hannah said. She dug into her rucksack and pulled out three invitations, each shaped like a witch's hat. She gave one each to Ellie, Payton and Amanda. "I've planned something fun. Have a look!"

Ellie flipped over the invitation. It read:

Grab your broom and bubbling brew!

Look what you're invited to:

A HALLOWEEN SLEEPOVER

WHERE: Hannah's house

WHEN: After we trick-or-treat!

"A sleepover?" Ellie asked. She took a small bite of her sandwich.

"That's right!" Hannah exclaimed. "My mum said it's OK because tomorrow is Saturday. We can play games, like Toilet Paper Mummy or Pin the Head on the Headless Horseman. And I've got mini pumpkins for us to paint. We'll have so much fun!"

Ellie's stomach filled with worry, and she lost her appetite. A sleepover at Hannah's meant facing the dark – without her lamp! She wondered if the dark made her friends nervous too.

"I'm going to wear my monster pyjamas," Payton said. "I got them for my birthday – with slippers that match."

Amanda held up her notebook. "I'll bring the scary story I've written. It's about a clumsy ghost that goes *bump* in the night. Get it?" She laughed.

No one is saying anything about the dark, Ellie thought as Amanda went on about her story. *Looks like I'm the only one who's afraid.*

"I have an idea!" Hannah added. "Let's watch a Halloween film, like *My Mad Science Project*." She looked at Ellie and smiled. "Tonight is going to be AMAZING!"

"Um, yeah!" Ellie replied, trying to sound excited. But truthfully, she wished the sleepover was already over. Her friends weren't scared of the dark like she was. Now she had to face her fear, or they might think she was a chicken.

Cluck! Ellie thought.

CHAPTER 3

Night-light fright

After school, Ellie sat on her bed staring at Hannah's invitation. She wanted to go to the sleepover more than anything. But how could she hide her fear from her friends?

Just then, Mum walked in with her lab coat. It was freshly cleaned and bright white. "Good news! My flower formula washed off," she said.

"The Ultra Washing Machine came to the rescue – again!"

Ellie smiled. Her parents' inventions always saved the day. There was the Ultra Scooperific, which had scooped up an army of mutant sweet wrappers. There was also the Ultra Rattle, which had no trouble getting a baby's attention. In fact, it had stopped a baby T-rex from devouring a milk lorry.

It was all in a day's work for Mum and Dad. They were super-genius scientists for BRAIN, a group tasked with catching super-villains.

As Mum handed over the lab coat, she spotted the invitation in Ellie's hand. "A sleepover! That will be fun!"

"Payton and Amanda are invited too," Ellie replied. "But I'm the only one who can't sleep in the dark."

"Why don't you take a torch?" Mum suggested. "There's one in our lab. We have all sorts of useful tools down there: torches, scissors, rulers, ecto-plasma-blasters . . ."

Ellie shook her head firmly. "Nobody else is scared. If I take that, I might as well dress up like a scaredy-cat."

"I see. . . ." Mum's voice faded as she watched Ellie put on the coat. Tapping her cheek thoughtfully, she said, "I have to get something from the lab." Then she disappeared out the door.

Faster than Ellie could say ecto-plasma-blasters, Mum returned with a bracelet. It beamed as brightly as Ellie's Princess Power lamp.

"Here's something else you can wear," she said. "A scientist invents things, so it can be your invention. It's called the Ultra Glow."

"The Ultra Glow?" Ellie squinted at the shining gadget. "Is it for BRAIN?"

"It's for *you*," Mum replied. "I made it just now. I dipped a piece of old jewellery into our ever-glow formula, so it will shine all night long." She slid the Ultra Glow onto Ellie's wrist. "You can use it as a night light. Your friends will think it's a part of your costume."

Ellie's face lit up. She could stay safe from the dark, and nobody would find out about her fear! "Thanks, Mum!" she said, throwing her arms around Mum's waist.

"Just remember," Mum added, "you don't need a gadget to conquer your fear. You already have the power to do that."

Mum helped Ellie finish getting ready. She let Ellie borrow her safety googles – another scientist must-have. Then they rolled Ellie's overnight things into a sleeping bag. Zipping into the kitchen, Ellie got her trick-or-treat sack from Dad.

"It's Ellie Ultra, Super Scientist," he said. He stepped back to admire her outfit, when suddenly, his Ultra Smartphone beeped.

"Attention, members of BRAIN," said an automated voice, "Fairy Frightmare has escaped."

Dad grabbed his phone from the table as Mum hurried over. Ellie flew behind them and peered at the screen, where a picture of a fairy had appeared. The fairy wore a shadowy dress and carried a bag of silver dust. Her wings twinkled like moonlight, and she flashed a naughty grin.

"Is that a super-villain?" Ellie asked.

"I'm afraid so," Dad replied. "Fairy Frightmare is the most magical mischief-maker in all of Winkopolis. She sprinkles sleeping citizens with her bad dream dust and traps them in nightmares about their worst fears."

"BRAIN caught the fairy last Halloween," Mum said. "But she must be on the loose again."

Ellie looked nervously at the picture. Fairy Frightmare sounded like a really bad villain. She used people's fears against them. "I wouldn't want to face her," she said.

"Don't worry, sweetie. BRAIN will catch that pesky pixie," Mum reassured her. She gave Ellie a small squeeze. "Have a great time at the sleepover. I can't wait to hear how your night went."

* * *

Ellie pushed Fairy Frightmare out of her mind as she took off for Hannah's. She had better things to think about. Tricks and treats and tonnes of spooky fun waited for her at the sleepover party!

Best of all, I don't need to worry about bedtime, Ellie thought, smiling at the Ultra Glow. The gadget shined on her wrist, brightening the night.

Hannah swung the door open when Ellie arrived. "Introducing Hannah the Ballerina!" she said. She spun around in a pretty tutu, then curtsied. "Ta-da!"

Payton and Amanda ran in from the other room. "Howdy, partner!" Payton greeted, waving a stick horse. She was dressed like a cowgirl.

Amanda wore a scarecrow costume. She had patches on her dungarees, and straw stuck out from beneath her sleeves. Tipping up her straw hat, she noticed the Ultra Glow. It peeked out from under Ellie's sleeve.

"Cool bracelet! Is that part of your costume?" Amanda asked.

Ellie nodded as everyone crowded around. "It's called the Ultra Glow," she explained, showing off the gadget. "My mum made it in her laboratory. But I'm pretending it's my invention."

"Wow! You look like a real scientist," Hannah said. She laced up her ballet slippers, then grabbed her trick-or-treating sack. "Now that we're all here, let's get started. Last one outside is a rotten apple!"

The friends hurried outside. They rang doorbells and collected stickers, lollipops, chocolate and popcorn. The night was full of treats – and thankfully no tricks.

Dex must have given up on surprising me, Ellie thought.

After a while, everyone's sack was stuffed. "These treats are heavy," Payton said. She leaned on her stick horse.

"I'm not sure I can carry one more thing," Ellie said. "My muscle power is mush!"

"Maybe that can be our last stop?" Hannah asked. She pointed to the house on the corner. In the garden, there was a skeleton with an eye patch and a hook for a hand. A skull-and-crossbones flag hung over the porch.

Everyone followed Hannah up the path. At the door, a treasure chest was brimming with bags of chocolate gold coins. A sign on the chest read: *Ahoy, matey! Please take one bag of "pirate loot"*.

The girls helped themselves, then skipped off the porch. As they passed the garden, a soft glow caught Ellie's super sight. A bag of glow-in-the-dark bracelets sat next to the skeleton.

Those bracelets look like the Ultra Glow, Ellie thought.

Suddenly, a twig snapped behind her. She turned and locked eyes with Dex's werewolf mask.

"Boo!" Dex shouted.

"Eep!" Ellie peeped. Her hands flew up, launching her sack skywards. Treats sailed out in every direction.

Dex howled louder than before. "Scared you again, Super Chicken!" he said. He flapped his arms and pecked the air. "Cluck, cluck, cluck!"

As he clucked away, Ellie swiped her sack off the ground. "That villain never gives up," she muttered.

"Dex is trouble times ten!" Hannah replied. She scrunched her eyebrows at Ellie's wrist. "Hey, where's your invention thingy?"

"Huh?" Ellie glanced down and gasped. The Ultra Glow was gone! It must've slipped off when she threw her treats!

In a blink, Ellie turned on her X-ray beams to search for the gadget. She scanned the garden, the

porch and even the treasure chest. No Ultra Glow. Her heart pounded. If she didn't find it, she'd be no match for the dark!

Just then Payton waved to her from near the skeleton. She had something in her hand. "Is this it?" she asked.

Ellie swooped over. Sure enough, Payton was holding what looked like the Ultra Glow. "Thanks, Payton!" Ellie said, slipping it on. "I thought I'd lost it." She breathed a big sigh of relief.

Quick as lightning, Ellie gathered the spilled treats. Then she left with her friends to begin the sleepover party. After all, with the Ultra Glow safely back on her wrist, she had no reason to fear the night.

CHAPTER 4

Friend freak-out

Back at Hannah's house, her mum greeted them with warm apple juice. They sipped juice around the kitchen table, painting pumpkins and listening to Amanda's ghost story.

When the story ended, Hannah announced, "Pyjama Time!" Everyone followed her upstairs to change.

Payton put on her monster pyjamas, and Amanda wore ones with stars. Ellie had brought her cosiest pyjamas. They had ruffles on the top and bottoms.

Hannah walked out of the bathroom wearing her cat nightdress. She was carrying rolls of toilet paper. "Before we watch a film, let's play Toilet Paper Mummy."

Ellie and Payton teamed up against Hannah and Amanda. "Ready, steady . . . GO!" Hannah shouted.

Heels blazing, Ellie raced around Payton, wrapping her in toilet paper. In five seconds flat, she had turned her friend into a two-ply mummy with extra absorbency.

"Mffwee mffwon!" Payton said. She pulled paper away from her mouth. "We won!"

Hannah dropped her roll. She had barely wrapped Amanda's ankle. "That was the fastest

game of Toilet Paper Mummy *ever*!" she said. "You both deserve a prize." She dug into her treat sack and took out some green slime for Ellie.

"This reminds me of my dad's radioactive jelly," Ellie said. "It jumped out of the jar and tried to eat Dad's toast. It was an experiment gone bad – *really* bad."

"And here's something for you, Payton." Hannah held out a rubber snake. It had beady eyes, a forked tongue and scales all over.

One look at the toy, and Payton nearly jumped out of her skin. "No way! You can keep that creepy thing," she said, backing away. "I'm scared of snakes."

"Scared?" Ellie made a surprised face.

Payton nodded. "I have been ever since I was little," she explained. "I was going down a tunnel slide when someone threw a rubber snake after me. It totally freaked me out. I thought it was chasing me!"

"Reptiles look scary," Ellie agreed. "But most of them are harmless. Take Cyclops, for example!" Cyclops was the Ultras' giant one-eyed iguana. He usually kept to himself, lounging on his rock and reading mystery novels.

"It sounds silly, I know," Payton said. "I'm probably the only one who's afraid of something."

"Not true," Amanda said. "I'm terrified of heights. I can't even use the climbing wall at the park. It's too high!"

"Sometimes I get stage fright," Hannah admitted. "I'll look at the audience and forget my routine! It makes me want to run off stage and hide." She lowered her eyes.

Amanda patted Hannah's shoulder. "You know your routine, perfectly," she said.

"I see you practise all the time. First you start with a pirouette . . ." She twirled with her hands above her head.

"And then you do an arabesque," Payton finished. She pointed her toes and stood on one leg, her arms out at her sides.

Hannah clapped as the girls bowed. "Thanks," she said. "If I can remember how my routine starts, then I'll be OK." She turned to Ellie and smiled weakly. "I'm sure superheroes aren't afraid of anything."

"Well . . ." Ellie paused while everyone waited for her answer. Her friends had talked about what made them afraid. Maybe sharing her fear wasn't a big deal. "I'm actually scared of the dark," she confessed.

"Whoa. Really?" Hannah replied. Payton and Amanda stared in disbelief.

Ellie nodded. "I can face any villain except the dark," she said. "Ever since I read this scary comic book I have to use a night light to go to bed. That's why I brought the Ultra Glow–"

Glancing at her wrist, Ellie stopped mid-sentence. The bracelet wasn't glowing. Suddenly she realized something. "Payton, where did you find my bracelet?" she asked.

"It was in that bag of bracelets at the last house," Payton replied. "You must have missed it."

Hannah leaned over and eyed the bracelet. "Is that thingy broken?"

Oh no, Ellie realized. *This isn't the real Ultra Glow. Payton grabbed the wrong bracelet!*

"I don't think this is the Ultra Glow," Ellie said slowly. "We must've taken one of the glow-in-the-dark bracelets instead."

Payton shrank a little at her mistake. "Oops! Sorry . . ."

"No problem! You can use my old night light." Hannah skipped to her desk drawer and took out a small light. On the front, there was a picture of a kitten in a basket.

Ellie brightened. There was no way the dark could get her now. "Thanks for saving me, Hannah," she replied.

After plugging the night light in, Hannah yawned. "I'm tired," she said. "Maybe we should skip the film?"

"It *is* getting late," Amanda agreed, looking at the clock.

The girls decided to settle down for the night. Hannah turned off the main light, and everyone climbed into their sleeping bags. They whispered and giggled until the room went quiet.

Ellie gazed at Hannah's night light on the wall. It burned brightly, melting her fear away. Bedtime was sure to be villain-free.

Suddenly, a tiny shadow fluttered overhead, and shimmering dust sprinkled down. But Ellie didn't notice, and neither did her friends. They were all sound asleep.

CHAPTER 5

Scary fairy

"ACHOO!" Ellie sneezed, her nose tickling. Rubbing it sleepily, she opened her groggy eyes and caught a glimpse of her hand. It shimmered with dust. "What is this stuff?"

Just then, Payton sat up and swiped at her pyjama top. She was covered in the same dust. "My monster pyjamas are sparkling!" she said.

Amanda and Hannah got to their feet and shook dust out of their hair. They were coated in sparkles too.

"Did we have a glitter fight?" Hannah asked.

"That's impossible!" Amanda shouted. "We're sleeping! Look!" She pointed at the floor, where everyone was fast asleep in the glow of Hannah's night light.

Ellie bent over her snoozing self. "Ellie? Ellie?" She clapped her hands to wake herself up, but the sleeping Ellie only yawned and rolled over.

"What's going on?" Hannah asked.

"Wink-weeds!" a tiny voice said. "Isn't it obvious? You're stuck in a dream!"

Ellie looked up and saw a fairy was fluttering overhead. She was no bigger than Ellie's Butterfly Girl action figure, with wings that twinkled.

"In fact, you are stuck in a *BAD* dream," the fairy continued. "And who put you there, you might ask? It was me, your magical mischief-maker . . . Fairy Frightmare!" Her shadowy dress rippled as she curtsied.

Ellie's eyes narrowed. The pint-sized pest was none other than BRAIN's escaped super-villain! "Let us go!" she shouted.

Fairy Frightmare laughed. "First, you must escape your fears," she said. "But it won't be easy with my bad dream dust. It turns *NIGHT* into a *FRIGHT*!" She pulled a handful of dust out of her bag and threw it onto Hannah's treat sack.

The sack moved one way, then the other. Suddenly, the rubber snake popped out! It slithered to the floor and began growing. Its tail grew longer. Its body grew wider. It got bigger and bigger until its head scraped the ceiling.

Payton stared at the scaly nightmare. Her mouth dropped open in terror. "S-S-S-SNAKE!" she cried.

The snake coiled around the girls and glared menacingly. Flicking its tongue, it let out a loud HISSSSS!

Ellie couldn't read a reptile's mind. But she could tell this one wasn't as friendly as Cyclops. "Let's get out of here!" she said.

The girls scrambled away as the snake lunged at their heels. They ran into the corridor and passed a bedroom where Hannah's mum was snoring softly. The snake slithered after them, snapping its massive jaws. It chased them down the stairs and out the door.

Ellie and her friends raced into the moonlight. Payton's fear seemed to give her a burst of super speed. She ran ahead, leading everyone down the street and into the park.

Rounding the tyre swing, the girls ducked for cover inside a kiddie play train. They crouched in the carriage as the snake glided past.

"Phew! I think it lost our trail," Payton said. She turned to Ellie hopefully. "Is it gone for good?"

Ellie shook her head. That snake was built to be bad, and bad guys never stopped causing trouble. Bullies like Dex had taught her that.

Payton cast a nervous look out of the window of the train carriage.

"Never mind the snake," Hannah said. "Who is Fairy Frightmare? Is she a villain? I promise I didn't invite any super-villains to my sleepover!"

"Fairy Frightmare escaped from BRAIN," Ellie explained. "She visits sleeping citizens and gives them nightmares about their fears."

Amanda slumped in her seat. "We'll never stop her," she grumbled. "How can we fight a fear?"

The same question was bugging Ellie. Suddenly – *Ka-ZAP!* – a thought supercharged her brainpower. She remembered what Mum had told her about fears.

"My mum said if you face your fear, you can conquer it," she replied. "You'll see it's not so scary."

"It looks scary to me!" Payton cried. Her hand shook as she pointed to the window. Peeking in were two huge snake eyes.

Seconds later . . . *FWOOMP!* The rubber reptile burst into the carriage. It charged after the girls as they raced through the train. Snapping at their ankles, it was gaining on them fast.

Time to stop this snake! Ellie thought. With blurring speed, she zoomed out of the train and circled around to the end. The snake's tail was sticking out of the window.

"Hold it right there, Scaly Pants!" Ellie ordered, grabbing the tail. She tugged with all her might and stopped the snake mid-slither.

Quickly Ellie's friends jumped out of the front train carriage. They ran across the playground towards the climbing wall. Just then, Fairy Frightmare flew out from behind the wall and sprinkled it with her bad dream dust.

"Climb out of your nightmare, if you can!" she sneered.

The climbing wall rumbled and shook. It spread out before the girls, stretching like an elastic band, until it went right across the horizon.

Payton got to the wall first. "Hurry! Let's get over this thing," she said. "The snake will be here any minute!"

As Hannah started climbing, Payton glanced back at Amanda curiously. Her friend hadn't moved. "C'mon, Amanda! What are you waiting for?"

Frozen with fear, Amanda stared at the wall. She was too scared of heights to climb it. It was as if she had come face-to-face with a giant mutant mouse.

"Help!" she squeaked.

CHAPTER 6

Wall of worry

"Stay put, Scales-for-Brains!" Ellie shouted. She held fast to the snake's tail as the snake wriggled inside the train. She couldn't let go of the toy terror, or Amanda was doomed. Just ahead, her friend was stuck at the climbing wall.

Things were not looking good.

Suddenly, the snake threw its rubber tail against the carriage window. *BOING!* Its body bounced around the frame. *BOING! BOING! BOING!*

"Whoooaa!" Ellie cried as the snake bucked like an angry bronco. It was trying to shake her off! She held on as tightly as she could, but her grip started to slip.

"Amanda, face your fear!" Ellie called to her friend. "It's the only way to escape!"

Amanda swayed dizzily as the wall loomed over her. It was normal-sized, but her fear made it seem taller than the Winkopolis clock tower. "Help!" she squeaked again.

"Help is here!" Payton said. She hopped down from the wall. "Grab a climbing hold. Then put one hand in front of the other. And keep your eyes forward."

"You can do it, Amanda!" Hannah cheered.

With a brave breath, Amanda unstuck her foot and stepped on the first climbing hold. She pulled herself up, then took another careful step. Payton and Hannah stayed at her side, giving pointers along the way.

Amanda climbed higher and higher. Before long, the wall didn't seem so tall.

Just then – *BOING!* – the snake's tail bounced once more. Ellie was catapulted into the air. Now free, the snake roared out of the train and charged across the park.

"Watch out!" Ellie cried.

Without a second to spare, the girls made their way to the top. They escaped over the edge as the snake raced up from behind. Momentarily defeated, it stopped at the wall and slid left and right like a caged cobra.

Ellie flew up and over the wall, landing safely on the other side. There, Amanda was standing tall.

"I did it! I conquered my fear of heights!" Amanda said proudly. "Bring on the next climbing wall . . . and the next . . . and the NEXT!" Holding her head high, she beamed.

Hannah and Payton cheered, but Ellie stayed quiet. Her supersonic ears had picked up a low rumble in the distance.

The climbing wall is shrinking! Ellie realized in a panic.

Now that Amanda had got over the wall, it was shrinking back to its normal size. In moments, nothing would stand between them and the rubber reptile.

Payton had to face her fear or they would be at its mercy!

"Payton, I know you're scared of the snake," Ellie said. "But your fear won't go away unless you stand up to it."

"How can I?" Payton cried, glancing nervously at the wall. It was getting shorter and shorter. "The snake is too big – and scaly!"

Before long, the wall ground to a halt. A long, forked tongue flicked out from one side. The friends moved back as the snake reappeared.

Amanda turned to Payton. "You have to stop that overgrown Halloween toy. Otherwise you'll be stuck running from it!"

"Stuck?" The fear on Payton's face slowly began to fade. "That's it! I *can* stop it," she said. "OK, I have a plan. Follow me!"

Sprinting away in her slippers, Payton led the girls to the other side of the playground. They ran under the monkey bars and headed straight for the climbing frame. A long tunnel slide curved around the frame. One after the other, they hurried up the ladder, their feet pounding on the steps.

When they reached the platform, Payton swung around and waved at the snake. "Over here! Come and get us!" she shouted.

Like a rocket, the snake shot across the playground. It rounded the climbing frame and wriggled up the ladder.

"Down the tunnel slide!" Payton said. One by one, the girls slid to safety. As the snake came up from behind, Payton turned to face her fear. "You can't catch me!" she said, then she disappeared into the dark tunnel.

With terrific force, the snake lunged after Payton. It could barely squeeze through the tunnel when . . . *THWUMP!* It was stuck!

At the bottom, the snake's head poked out. Payton looked straight into its beady eyes and stuck out her tongue. "You're not so scary now," she said.

With that, the snake shrank back into a harmless toy. Just then, Fairy Frightmare fluttered down from a lamp post. The super-villain looked like she was in a very bad mood. "You may have fought those fears, but I'm not finished," she told the girls. "I have a new fright for you!"

The pixie scooped out a mound of bad dream dust and flung it into the sky. It fell over the landscape like a shimmering mist, changing everything it touched. The sky became a ceiling with spotlights. The park faded as four walls rose from the ground. The walls connected to make an enormous auditorium.

A floor formed beneath Ellie's feet. Then – *SPROING!* – a chair sprang up underneath her.

Rows and rows of chairs popped up, filling the rest of the space. Each one had an audience member.

Payton and Amanda were sitting next to Ellie. "Hey, where's Hannah?" Payton asked, scanning the audience curiously. "She was here a minute ago."

The girls glanced around as the spotlights blinked on. The lights directed their attention to a stage with a beautiful velvet curtain.

Suddenly, music filled the air. "Introducing Hannah the Ballerina!" a voice announced.

The curtain parted, and there was Hannah. She wore her dance costume, but she didn't seem to be in a dancing mood. She was as stiff as a statue, her eyes focused on the audience.

If Ellie hadn't known better, she would've thought Hannah had been zapped by the Ultra

Statue Creator. But Ellie knew for a fact that it was locked in Mum and Dad's laboratory.

Something even more powerful had struck her best friend.

Ellie gasped. "Stage fright!"

CHAPTER 7

All eyes on Hannah

Hannah stood in the glare of the spotlight. Hundreds of eyes stared back at her. As Ellie watched, Hannah's face turned pea-soup green. It looked like she had eaten too many jack-o'-lantern pizzas for lunch. Stage fright clearly had a hold on Hannah.

How can we help her break free? Ellie thought.

There was only one way to find out. Ellie activated her mind-reading power to peek into Hannah's head.

Inside, it was messy. Hannah was trying to remember her dance routine, but her mind flickered like a glitchy computer screen. It was hard to see how the routine went.

Amanda spun around in her seat. "Why isn't Hannah moving?" she asked Ellie and Payton.

"Shhh! The show is about to start," a woman scolded them. She put a finger to her lips, then turned back towards the stage.

Ellie leaned close to her friends. "Hannah has forgotten her routine," she whispered. "She's trying to remember the moves, but her mind is all scrambled. It's like a ham and cheese omelette in there!"

"If Hannah doesn't perform, this nightmare will never end!" Payton said. "Do you think we can dance in her place? Or is that cheating?"

Ellie doubted they could take Hannah's place. Fairy Frightmare wouldn't let them get away with that.

"Hannah has to conquer her own fear," she replied. "But there must be some way we can help. . ."

Just then, an idea leaped across Ellie's brain waves like a high-flying ballerina. She whispered her idea to Payton and Amanda. After blinking herself invisible, she took off for the stage.

Ellie landed at her friend's side, but no one could see her. Thanks to her invisibility power, she was as hidden as a polar bear in a snowstorm.

"Hannah, it's Ellie," she whispered.

"Ellie?" Hannah blinked twice. "Help! I'm not sure how to begin my routine. I can't think straight – not with everyone watching me!" Her eyes skimmed over the crowd, and she took a step back. She took another step, then another. . .

Hannah was going to run off stage!

"You know your routine by heart," Ellie said, trying to settle her friend's nerves. "You just need a reminder." She zipped to the ceiling and pointed a spotlight towards the back of the auditorium.

The light hit Amanda and Payton. They were waiting behind the last row, ready to perform. On Ellie's signal, the girls pirouetted. Then they each stood on one leg, their toes pointed. Lifting their other legs, they extended their arms into a graceful arabesque.

Hannah's mind cleared as she watched her friends. "That's it!" she cried. "Now I remember!"

At once, Hannah came alive on stage. She pirouetted. She arabesqued. She swayed left and right like a paper ghost in the wind. The music played as she tiptoed in figures of eight, then took a lovely leap, sweeping her toes across the stage.

Hannah was so busy dancing that she didn't even notice the audience. It was only after her performance that she looked up. She smiled as everyone roared with applause. Roses rained down around her.

Ellie floated onto the stage while Amanda and Payton came running.

"I got over my stage fright!" Hannah told them, her recital costume fading. Soon she was back in her cat nightdress. "Thanks for helping me remember what to do."

"No problem!" Payton said. "In a way, ballet dancing is like playing football. There's lots of moving around. You don't end up with grass stains, though."

Suddenly – *CLICK!* – a spotlight went out overhead. Seconds later, more lights went out. *CLICK . . . CLICK . . . !*

Amanda looked confused as the room slowly dimmed. "The lights are turning off by themselves," she said. "Is it magic?"

"It's *fairy* magic!" Ellie cried. She pointed overhead. Fairy Frightmare was sprinkling her bad dream dust on the lights, turning them off one by one. "That sprite is up to something sinister!"

Fairy Frightmare flew up to the last spotlight. "You haven't stopped me!" she squeaked at the girls. "If you think those fears were bad, wait until you see what's next. It's stronger than a superhero!" Her eyes zeroed in on Ellie. "Try to fight *THIS* fright."

With an itty-bitty breath, the fairy blew some dust at the light. Instantly, it went out. Everything plunged into darkness.

"Hello-o-o?" Ellie's voice echoed in the murky void that surrounded her. It seemed to travel far into the distance. "Is anybody there?"

No one answered.

"Hannah?" Ellie called. "Amanda? Payton?" She blinked on her X-ray vision, hoping to shed some light on their whereabouts. She scanned up and down and left and right. But they were nowhere to be seen.

Just then, a biting wind blew through. It nipped at Ellie while whooshing past. Yes, her friends were gone. But Ellie's super senses told her she wasn't alone.

The wind started to swirl around. It picked up speed, sucking in the darkness. Something wild and hairy took shape. It appeared to be a beast – the same sort of beast that ate superheroes for supper.

Ellie swallowed hard. "The dark!"

CHAPTER 8

Ellie vs the dark

AWHOOOO! The beast let out a terrible howl and came into view. It was a dark, shadowy creature with spiky hair and fangs that would give even Dracula a fright. And it was straight out of Ellie's bad dream.

Ellie backed away, her heart racing. "I'm not afraid. I'm not afraid. . ." she repeated, trying desperately to gather her courage. But in truth, she felt like a big chicken. It didn't help that the creature looked at her like she was a drumstick.

Chomping its teeth, the beast lunged.

"Yikes!" Ellie cried. She weaved around the beast's jaws of doom like a fast-footed footballer. She ducked left. She dived right. But her speed didn't slow it down.

I have to fight my fear, but how? Ellie wondered.

Could she use her super strength? No. The dark was a swirling shadow. Smashing it would be impossible. How about her heating power? Not a chance! The shadow would blow out her fired-up fists like candles on a cake!

Ellie's fear wasn't an ordinary, everyday villain. It couldn't be squished or cooked or kicked out of Earth's orbit. Her superpowers were useless against it.

I'm powerless! she thought.

Frightened, Ellie blinked herself invisible. Her ears pounded while she listened to the beast sniffing for her.

Just then, Mum's words echoed in Ellie's head: *"You don't need superpowers to fight your fear. You just have to face it. . ."*

Ellie trembled at the thought. *But I can't. The dark will eat me up. I don't want to be a midnight snack!*

Her stomach flooded with worry and weighed her down. She sank to the ground, feeling helpless.

Suddenly Ellie heard voices:

"Stand up, Ellie! Stand up to the dark!"

"It won't seem so scary. C'mon, you can do it!"

"We fought our fears! You can too!"

It was Ellie's friends. She couldn't see them, but she could hear them. They were there, encouraging her to be brave. Ellie realized she was letting her fear overpower her. If she was going to take back that power, she had to choose not to be afraid.

In that moment, something stirred inside her. It was a mighty feeling, mightier than all her super powers put together. It made her feel like she could face anything – slimy sludge, rowdy robots . . . even the dark!

With a strength she'd never felt before, Ellie reappeared as the creature closed in. "Go away!" she shouted. "I gave you power. But now I'm taking it back. I'm not afraid of you!"

The beast threw back its head and howled. *AWHOOOO!* The wind picked up again. It whirled around the beast, pulling in more and more darkness.

The beast doubled, then tripled in size. It grew and grew until it surrounded Ellie. Its eyes glared down at her and threatened to swipe her bravery.

Ellie fought to stay strong. "I'm not afraid!" she yelled as the wind whipped through her hair. "I've stopped super-villain invasions!" She stuck her hands on her hips and stood boldly. "I can stop you too!"

Opening its mouth wide, the beast revealed rows of razor-sharp teeth.

This is it. I'm Super Chicken Stew! Ellie thought. She braced herself for the worst, but to her surprise, her fear began fading.

Slowly the beast shrank away like a bashful cloud. It grew smaller before disappearing into thin air. Eventually the only thing left was plain old darkness, which no longer seemed that scary.

Moments later, Ellie found herself back in Hannah's room.

"Ellie, you conquered the dark!" Hannah cheered. She was standing there with Amanda and Payton. "We knew you could do it!"

Ellie smiled. "Thanks," she said. "That was the closest I've come to being eaten by a villain. Unless you count the time a robo-whale almost swallowed me . . ."

"Snuggle-snails!" a pixie voice piped up.

The girls turned and saw Fairy Frightmare pouting on Hannah's pillow. It looked like she had got out of the wrong side of the bed. "I will not be defeated," the grumpy villain complained.

Ellie marched over. "No more bad dreams!" she said. "We squashed our fears. You have to let us go!"

"That's right," Payton replied, stepping forward. "You've run out of stuff that will scare us."

"You think so, do you?" A crooked grin spread across the fairy's face. Clearly she had something wicked brewing.

Fairy Frightmare opened her bag of bad dream dust and held it out for everyone to see. "Have a look, if you dare!" she said.

Nervously, the girls peeked into the bag. The dust sparkled with frightening images. There were creepy dolls, a ghost in the attic, no break time and other things designed to make kids squirm.

This is what nightmares are made of, Ellie thought.

Fairy Frightmare scooped out some dust. Hundreds of grains slipped through her little fingers. "I carry many fears. Some fears will make you shiver, and others will curl your hair," she said.

"If you can fight them, I will let you out of this bad dream."

"But what if we can't?" Amanda asked.

The fairy laughed a no-good laugh. "Then you will be stuck in a never-ending nightmare!"

CHAPTER 9

What is a villain afraid of?

Fairy Frightmare threw bad dream dust on the ground. It quickly sprouted into an army of small leafy cabbages . . . with teeth.

"It's man-eating brussels sprouts!" Ellie cried. She jumped back as the carnivorous vegetables marched towards her. Usually she only took on brussels sprouts at dinner time.

Payton turned to the other girls. "I can handle this fear," she said. "They look like mini footballs. A few kicks should show them who's boss!"

Racing up to the mean greens, Payton swung her leg hard. *Fwoom! Fwoom! Fwoom!* She kicked away the veggies before they could take a bite out of her slippers.

The brussels sprouts flew across the room and faded away. Quickly Fairy Frightmare reached into her bag. She dropped more dust on the floor, and a familiar figure sprang up like a pogo-stick.

Ellie's eyebrows shot towards the ceiling. It was Miss Little, their class teacher!

Miss Little tapped a ruler firmly against her palm. It looked like she meant business – homework business. "For your homework, you will write a poem," she said. "It must be twenty pages long, single-spaced."

"That's easy!" Amanda replied. "I can write a poem in my sleep."

She sat down at a desk that appeared in front of her and got out her notebook. Lines poured from Amanda's pencil. As she wrote, Miss Little slowly began to disappear.

With a frown, Fairy Frightmare dug out even more dust. "Here's a *MONSTER* of a fear!" she squeaked. She threw the silver grains under Hannah's bed.

Hannah gasped as a long tentacle slid out from beneath the bed. An octopus creature emerged, covered with hundreds of blinking eyes.

"It's Googly!" she cried. "I used to have nightmares that it lived under my bed when I was younger."

The monster wriggled towards Hannah. It was trying to scare her off, but she didn't budge.

"I'm not afraid of you, Googly!" she said. "Get back under the bed, right now." She lifted her foot and gave one of the octo-arms a serious stomp.

Squealing, the monster retreated. Fairy Frightmare glared as it slunk out of sight. Furious, she stuck her hand into her bag, scooped out as much dust as she could hold, and dropped the bag on the ground.

"I'm going to fill this place with fears," she declared. "You'll never be able to conquer them all!"

Fairy Frightmare fluttered over the girls and stopped in the middle of the room. She took a whopping breath and blew the dust in every direction.

Fears popped up everywhere. There were barking dogs and screeching bats. There was a mummy crawling out of its tomb. There was even a newspaper with the terrifying headline, *SUMMER HOLIDAYS CANCELLED.*

A lumpy ogre appeared in front of Ellie. It leaned over her and snorted, its breath stinking like sweaty socks.

Ogre breath is a nightmare! Ellie thought, pinching her nose.

The fears closed in on Ellie and her friends. They couldn't fight every fear. And even if they could, there were lots more waiting in the bag of bad dreams. It held the fairy's power. If they were going to escape, Ellie had to take that power away.

Ellie's super sight locked onto the bag. It was sitting on the floor. The fairy hovered over it, cackling with delight. Fairy Frightmare was so busy enjoying the mayhem she'd created that she'd forgotten about it.

Now's my chance! Taking off at top speed, Ellie rocketed past fear after fear. She flew through a ghostly graveyard and ducked a flying spaceship. When the villain wasn't looking, she snatched the bag.

Ellie was about to run off with it when – *Ka-POW!* – an idea struck her. Maybe she could use the fears against Fairy Frightmare!

Her eyes scanned the grains for the perfect fright. It had to be something that a villain was afraid of, but what? Spelling tests? The dentist?

Aha! Ellie poured some dust into her hand. *This is it!*

With a flick of her wrist, Ellie sprinkled it over Fairy Frightmare. Suddenly wire-thin bars cascaded like a waterfall around the super-villain.

They anchored to a platform that appeared under her feet. In no time, the fairy was trapped in a birdcage.

"Wait, what's this? I've been caught?" The fairy stopped laughing. "But that's impossible! I just broke free from BRAIN!"

As Fairy Frightmare darted around the cage like a wild hummingbird, Ellie ran to her trick-or-treat sack. She opened the sack and dumped out the goodies.

"This nightmare is officially over!" Ellie declared. She scooped the fairy, cage and all, into her sack.

At once, fears began to disappear. Now that the villain had lost her power, they faded away for good.

Hannah sighed with relief. "Phew! I've fought enough frights for one night," she said.

Payton nodded in agreement. "I'm glad the fears are gone."

"And they won't come back," Ellie added. She held the bag of bad dream dust in one hand and grasped her trick-or-treat sack in the other. "Fairy Frightmare has finished making mischief."

The sack flailed around. Inside, the fairy was trying to break free.

"Set me free!" she cried in a muffled voice. "I promise to give you a good dream. Maybe one with a zombie apocalypse? Wait . . . no! That's bad. I mean, how about a dream with rainbows? Or puppies? *OR RAINBOW PUPPIES?*"

Ellie shook her head. She doubted Fairy Frightmare would keep a promise like that. Once an evil villain, always an evil villain.

"How did you stop the fairy anyway?" Amanda asked. "I thought this nightmare would never end!"

Ellie tied the sack with a super-tight knot.
"I used the fear that scares villains the most,"
she replied. "Getting caught. It's a villain's worst
nightmare."

CHAPTER 10

Extra power

Morning light brightened Hannah's room. Ellie blinked open her tired eyes and squinted at the sunrise.

"It's morning already?" She yawned. "I feel like I've hardly slept."

Payton gave a waking-up stretch. "Me too," she replied. "I wonder if it's because of my dream.

I was running from a giant rubber snake." She laughed. "It sounds crazy, doesn't it?"

"Wait, I remember that!" Hannah jumped out of her sleeping bag. She went to her desk and grabbed her trick-or-treat sack off the chair. "It was *this* snake, wasn't it?" She pulled out the Halloween toy.

The toy dangled in front of Payton, but surprisingly, it didn't seem to bother her. "In my dream, I was so scared of that thing," she said. "But it's nothing to be afraid of, really. . ."

Payton paused and looked at Hannah. "Hey! How do you know what I dreamed about?"

Amanda gasped, and everyone glanced over. "We were trapped in the same dream, *that's* how!" she replied. "It was all about fighting our fears. They came from that villain – the one that crashed our sleepover party. Fairy What's-Her-Face!"

"Fairy Frightmare. . ." Ellie said slowly.

Her fuzzy memories started coming into focus: BRAIN's warning, the bad-dream dust, the snake chase, scaling the wall and Hannah's stage fright. Even the beastly dark! She also remembered using the fairy's magic against her.

Is it true? Ellie wondered. *Did I actually catch that villain?*

"Cosy-cobwebs!" a quiet voice squeaked. "Let me out of this jail. Night will come again, and I need to scare the city's sleepyheads!"

Ellie turned and saw her treat sack bouncing around like a robo-bunny. Lollipops, chocolate, caramel squares and other goodies were scattered nearby.

"Amanda's right!" Ellie exclaimed. She zipped over and triumphantly picked up the sack. "We fought our fears and won!"

"Wow, I've never defeated a villain before," Hannah said. Her eyes widened. "It makes dancing in front of an audience look easy-peasy."

"I suppose the climbing wall isn't that bad, either," Amanda said. "I have an idea! Let's go to the park, and I'll climb it again. In real life, this time!" She turned as Ellie picked up the fairy's bag of dust. "How about it, Ellie?"

Ellie shook her head. "I'd better take Fairy Frightmare to my parents," she replied. "BRAIN needs to know she's been caught. That way everyone can rest easy."

Ellie got out her clothes, and in a flash she was dressed. Then she gathered up her stuff and said goodbye to her friends. It had been a fright-filled night for all of them, but she was glad they had powered through it together.

* * *

Rooftops blurred below as Ellie flew home. She was almost there when a soft glow caught her eye. It was coming from the house where she'd lost the Ultra Glow.

It couldn't be, Ellie thought. *Could it?*

She swooped down for a closer look and landed in the front garden. Sure enough, the gadget was shining in the bag of glow-in-the-dark bracelets. The light from the other bracelets had gone out, making the Ultra Glow easy to spot.

"I found it!" Ellie cried, slipping it on. It was good to have the bracelet back. It wasn't one of Mum and Dad's mighty inventions, but it still made her feel extra powerful.

With the Ultra Glow back on her wrist and Fairy Frightmare in hand, Ellie took off again. Before long, she was trudging through her front door.

"Hopefully bad guys will be on their best behaviour today," Ellie said to herself. "I'm too tired to battle anybody. I need a nap first."

"Ellie's home!" Mum exclaimed. She watched as Ellie rubbed her eyes, and her smile faded. "Uh-oh," she said. "Looks like our do-gooder didn't get a good night's sleep. . ."

Just then, Super Fluffy raced around the corner to greet Ellie. He stopped at her treat sack and started to growl.

"I didn't sleep very well," Ellie confessed. "I was busy catching this villain."

She shined her X-ray beams on the sack and revealed the villain inside. The fairy was sitting with her arms crossed, pouting.

"Fairy Frightmare?" Dad exclaimed. "How did you find her? BRAIN searched the entire city!"

Ellie handed over Fairy Frightmare and

her bad dream dust. "She came to Hannah's sleepover," she explained. "She trapped us all in the same nightmare, and we had to fight off her frights. It was hard, but we escaped."

Mum hugged Ellie. "I'm glad you're safe," she said. "Did the dark give you any trouble? If it did, I hope the Ultra Glow helped."

"I didn't need it after all," Ellie said. "Fighting the dark was tough, but you were right. Its power came from me. I decided not to be afraid, and it made me stronger than ever! My fear didn't stand a chance."

Dad eyed the Ultra Glow. "If you don't want that bracelet, maybe we can put it to use," he said. "The Mad Gopher is digging up our garden again. That villain hides underground, so it's hard to find him. The Ultra Glow can shine a light on his hiding place."

Ellie was about to take off the bracelet for Dad when she stopped. "Actually, I think I'll keep it, if that's OK. . ." She headed upstairs as her parents exchanged knowing glances.

In her room, Ellie swept her Princess Power comic book off her bed. She flicked through the pages and spotted glimpses of the beast from her nightmare. Her fear started to creep back.

"I'm not afraid," she reminded herself.

Ellie returned the comic to her bookcase and put the Ultra Glow next to her lamp. She smiled at the shining bracelet. She knew she had the power to conquer her fear – but having a little extra power never hurt.

GLOSSARY

arachnid group of animals that includes spiders and scorpions

bronco wild horse from western North America

carnivorous meat-eating

conquer successfully overcome a weakness or problem

glitchy having an unexpected, usually minor, problem

high jinks wild or rowdy behaviour

ogre ugly giant from fairy tales and folklore that eats people

sinister especially evil or leading to evil

sprite elf or fairy

tomb house or burial chamber for dead people

TALK ABOUT ELLIE!

1. At bedtime, Ellie faces a fearsome villain – the dark! Talk about a time when you were scared. What were you afraid of? How did you cope with your fear?

2. Ellie doesn't want her friends to know she is afraid of the dark. She worries they will think she is a chicken. What would you say to Ellie to ease her worries?

3. Ellie, Hannah, Amanda and Payton are good friends. They encourage each other to stand up to their fears. They even battle a super-villain together! Talk about some other things that good friends do together.

EXPRESS YOURSELF!

1. Ellie's mum creates the Ultra Glow to help Ellie fight the dark. Pretend you're a super-genius scientist and draw a picture of an invention that could help squash Ellie and her friends' fears. Then write a paragraph explaining how your invention works.

2. Amanda wrote a story about a clumsy ghost that goes bump in the night. It's your turn to write a ghost story. When you've finished, share it with a friend or your teacher. Boo!

3. The girls play games, including Toilet Paper Mummy, at Hannah's sleepover party. Make up a game to play with your friends or family at Halloween. Don't forget a spooky prize for the winner!

ABOUT THE AUTHOR

Gina Bellisario is an ordinary grown-up who can do many extraordinary things. She can make things disappear, such as a cheeseburger or a grass stain. She can create a masterpiece out of glitter glue and shoelaces. She can even thwart a messy room with her super cleaning power! Gina lives in Illinois, USA, with her husband and their super kids.

ABOUT THE ILLUSTRATOR

Jessika von Innerebner loves creating – especially when it inspires and empowers others to make the world a better place. She got her first illustration job at the age of seventeen and hasn't looked back since. Jess is an illustrator who loves humour and heart and has coloured her way through projects with Disney.com, Nickelodeon, Fisher-Price and Atomic Cartoons, to name a few. In her spare moments, Jess can be found long-boarding, yoga-ing, dancing, adventuring to distant lands and laughing with friends. She currently lives in sunny Kelowna, Canada.

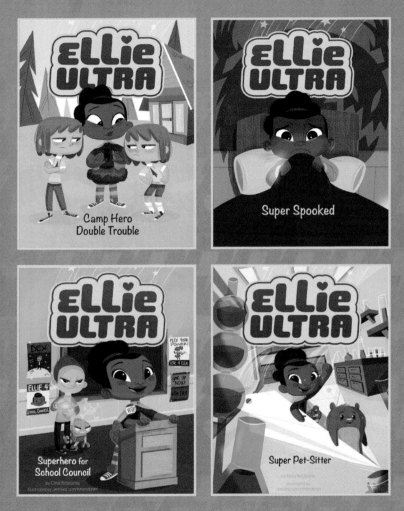

ONLY FROM RAINTREE!

THE FUN DOESN'T STOP HERE!

Discover more at *www.raintree.co.uk*